Jo-Ann Ong studied law at the University of Sheffield from 1990 to 1993 and acquired a master's degree in Banking Law from Boston University in 1994. During her free time, she enjoys piano playing and looking after her pets. She lives in Melbourne and has recently completed a master's degree in International Relations from Monash University.

I would like to dedicate this book to T.T.

Jo-Ann Ong

DAS EINZIGE KIND / THE ONLY CHILD

AUSTIN MACAULEY PUBLISHERS®

LONDON ∙ CAMBRIDGE ∙ NEW YORK ∙ SHARJAH

A CIP catalogue record for this title is available from the British Library.

ISBN 9781035876044 (Paperback)
ISBN 9781035876051 (Hardback)
ISBN 9781035876075 (ePub e-book)
ISBN 9781035876068 (Audiobook)

www.austinmacauley.com

First Published 2024
Austin Macauley Publishers Ltd®
1 Canada Square
Canary Wharf
London
E14 5AA

Character names in the story

Christian, protagonist
Amelia, Christian's sister
Sabina, Christian's filming agent
Manfred, Sabina's ex-boyfriend
Tatiana, Yolanda's aunt
Yolanda, Christian's girlfriend
Siegfried, Christian's boss
Katharina, Yolanda's colleague, intern
Ulrich, scriptwriter
Henrique, bookstore owner
Ned, doctor
Penelope, receptionist
Babak, Amelia's chauffeur
Lorenzo, train conductor

Chapter 1

It was a beautiful summer's day. Christian left his apartment and he made his way to the studio in the white building by train. Christian lived near the city centre. He had a girlfriend called Yolanda who lives in the same apartment block. In the studio in the white building, actors are seen taking auditions in the office and on set. Christian had read the note taped to the building and he was eager to see how he could play a role in the movie. He was a budding actor and worked as a scientist at the time. Sabina, who worked at the reception, saw Christian walking into the office. She said, "How are you? Can I help you?"

Christian replied, "I would like to attend the audition for the role at a friend's wedding. Do you have any good ideas where I can find a wedding venue for that audition?"

Sabina looked at him up and down and said, "I can't say that because you need to read the messages in these notes first. Here, take these notes, then hurry up and pay attention to the traffic."

Christian replied, "Thank you very much." He hurried to the venue where he saw a lot of cameramen and a director conducting the audition. Christian read the audition notes and prepared himself for the audition.

Meanwhile, it was almost lunchtime when the audition ended. Sabina went for a walk on the street, in a good mood. She suddenly saw a blue ring lying on the stone. She was very surprised because it looked beautiful. *It belongs to a woman. Maybe she will look at it again after a while. I would leave it alone*, she thought. Sabina walked on. After a day at the office, she was walking home. She found a blue ring on the floor but didn't know that it was placed there by her ex-boyfriend, Manfred. Sabina walked on. The sun went behind the black clouds and disappeared. The atmosphere became windy and chilly.

At the very same time, Christian was carrying a heavy bag, and he was looking for a store in the market. It was raining, and he saw a significant and one of the oldest buildings in town where people were staying. He was very disappointed by the audition. He would not have a good chance of becoming a showman. He strolled as it was raining. Christian went into a bookstore that he visited regularly. He was looking for a magazine. He was on good terms with the store owner, Heinrique. "We are closed," said Heinrique.

"Excuse me. Do you have the latest magazine?" asked Christian.

"What are you looking for?" asked Heinrique.

"The magazine featuring the latest editor's comments," says Christian.

Heinrique handed a magazine to Christian and said, "Here, take this. This is last week's magazine. You'll get the latest magazine in at least two weeks' time."

Christian said, "Thank you." Christian took the magazine and headed home. Heinrique was the owner of one of the oldest bookstores in Munich, Germany. He was a political man and fervently supported his own political party. Christian knew of his political ambitions which he had pursued.

Meanwhile, it was ten o'clock in the evening. Sabina was at home. Her apartment had a large window, two bedrooms, a small kitchen and a bathroom. Her rent is $1,540.00 per month. In order to pay for the higher rent, she would work in the evening in a nearby library. Earlier in the morning, she would have a dull day. As the ring did not belong to anyone, she returned from the library to the street at eight o'clock in the night and saw the same ring still lying on the stone. She picked up the ring and put it in her handbag. Now the ring was on her desk in her apartment. She considered who the ring might belong to for a little while and then went to bed. It was almost eleven o'clock in the night.

The next morning, Christian woke up early. He went to the kitchen and drank water. He cannot find anyone nearby. His neighbour, Yolanda had left the apartment. The building in which he lived had five floors. Yolanda lived on the third floor. Her aunt, Tatiana, lived alone in an apartment on the street level. Although she was an older woman, she still worked for a shop in the same office as Sabina. Christian did not know her aunt on a personal basis. Christian went to the market again. He was feeling a bit anxious. The magazine he got last night did not have a nomination for his scientific article. He remembered the audition that happened last night. The movie director had said that Christian was too young. Christian thought that as soon as he danced, he would get the part. However, he is not a showman. The other actors and actresses were mostly old people. They danced slowly, unlike Christian, who did not keep to the rhythm. Worst of all, he had no partner. When he danced, all the older people laughed because he danced in a funny way. "You have to practise more dancing," said an older man. Christian was annoyed by the bad reception and was very embarrassed. In five minutes, he had left the audition. Christian knew that he had to remain strong in his career as a budding actor. He could not let criticism dampen his spirits. He knew that he had to be stoic and at the same time, persevering.

Meanwhile, when Sabina picked up the ring from the street, she did not see a man, Manfred hiding in the bushes. The ring belonged to Manfred. However, he did not follow Sabina as it was late in the evening. As the night light was not intense, he went home instead. Manfred felt a little sad. He has no family because he is unemployed. Throughout the day, he sat in a cafe. He usually read the newspapers and drank a few beers. Last night he saw the ring on the street which he put it on the stone. He did not take it back because it was too blue and beautiful. In her bedroom, Sabina thought for a moment. "The ring isn't mine," she finally said. Then she slept.

When she woke up, she ate breakfast and then went to the market. By chance, she saw a young man, Christian. He walked quickly and did not smile. *That is bad*, he thought in an annoyed mood. *My article has not been chosen and is not in the magazine yet*, he thought. Although he was not as disappointed as yesterday, he felt surprised because he suddenly saw Sabina arriving in the marketplace. Sabina went into a museum. In a few minutes, she came out in a frustrated mood. She saw Christian, who was standing opposite her. He had a surprised look. "Hello," he said.

"Hello," said Sabina.

"The play which I attended yesterday in the audition. It was a total catastrophe," said Christian.

"I'm sorry. I have to hurry. I cannot talk now. Here, take this," said Sabina as he handed Christina the blue ring. In a split second of the moment, Sabina ran away. Meanwhile, Manfred had seen Sabina talking to Christian. He jumped up from his chair and walked quickly out of the cafe. He ran behind Christian and shouted. Christian felt a big panic and gave him the ring. Christian leaves in a hurry. Christian has seen Manfred before a couple of times at the studio where he is seen chatting up Sabina. He knew that the ring did not belong to Sabina either and the best thing he could have done at that juncture was to return it to Manfred.

Meanwhile, Sabina was in the office. She was talking to Tatiana, her colleague. Sabina realized that Christian thought he did not get the part in the film. She asked Tatiana's niece, Yolanda to give him the program. "Do you know the man?" asked Sabina.

"Who?" asked Tatiana. Tatiana looks at the program sheet and sees Christian's name and photo. "That's my niece's boyfriend," said Tatiana.

"Are you sure?" asked Sabina.

"A hundred per cent," said Tatiana.

"Please give him this program sheet," said Sabina.

"Sure," said Tatiana.

Both women worked in silence for a while. Then, Sabina goes out of the room. Tatiana texted Yolanda after Sabina walked out of the room. She mentioned Christian's name and that he had got the part in the audition yesterday. She also said that she had a program sheet for him. Yolanda texted back to say that she would pass Christian the program sheet after she had seen Tatiana this afternoon. The play was to be scheduled for next week. Christian had practised a few dance moves and he feels very cheerful now that he knew that he got the part in the play. When the next week arrived, Christian was dancing in a part of the stage play. The entire play was filmed with the director who sat as one of the audience. *Christian danced well but a little too fast*, thought Yolanda. Meanwhile, one of his scientific articles had been accepted by the editor of the scientific journal. Both Christian and Yolanda were very happy with the comments from the editor. They felt satisfied. Although this was the first time his article had been accepted in the magazine, and he was a newcomer in the magazine, he was happy that the readers had finally accepted his article.

Chapter 2

Two years later, Christian got a job as a scientist and he went to work every day in the office. His office had a table, two large windows, a chair and a wooden floor. Christian read a book called 'The Beautiful World' because he was interested in science. An hour later, Christian went for a walk in the street again. He bought a newspaper and smoked a cigarette. As he walked, he thought about his mother, who lived in another city. What do you do for a living, his girlfriend, Yolanda, once asked because she was curious. I write, he replied, when I want to. In the night, Christian was doing some work in the laboratory where he found a development of findings. Christian was alone, and he tried to develop a theory. Suddenly, a man walked out of the building. *How did you get in here*, he thought because it was almost ten o'clock in the evening. He heard the man shouting. Then the man ran on foot, for he had quick steps. Christian was curious as to the identity of the man, but he did not make any noise. No one could be heard. Suddenly, the whole building was darkened. Then the man went back on foot. In a while, he was gone. Christian decides to go home and is back at home in half an hour. When Christian was home, he remembered the mysterious man near the laboratory room, so he was surprised.

Because it was late at night, however, he did not expect to hear anyone at that hour of the night. Then, he did some housekeeping. It was almost midnight. After taking a shower, he slept for the whole night. He woke up at seven the following day. Christian strolls to the bus stop. He felt exhausted. His girlfriend, Yolanda, had woken up early and gone to work. She made no noise. Where he was standing at the bus stop, he could see a building in the distance that had an ancient view. He was waiting for the bus. It was raining. He got on the bus. He saw no one in the street. Christian reached the office in about forty minutes' time. He read the newspapers in his office. His boss walked into the building. He was in a bad mood. Suddenly, a book fell to the floor. Christian was shocked. He took a quick look at the window. He saw that it was pouring rain. Then his boss, Siegfried, an older man, went into Christian's office. He was drenched. He looked at him with a sad but bored expression.

"Come with me to the laboratory room," he said to Christian.

Siegfried, Christian's boss, talked to him in the laboratory room. "Good morning," said Christian.

"Where were you last night?" asks Siegfried.

"What happened?" asks Christian.

"The window was wide opened and there was a sleeping man in the doorway," said Siegfried.

"That's none of my business," said Christian finally.

"You should make sure that all the colours are changed. The calculation doesn't match," said Siegfried.

"I'll go at once," said Christian. Christian quickly ran to the old building where the laboratory was.

Christian picks up the inventory. He sits down on the chair and looks very introspective. Meanwhile, he drinks a cup of tea. He was not at all enthusiastic. He was asked to improve the situation, but he felt he had to. In fact, he felt that he was compelled to do so. It was part of his nature, as he was a perfectionist. It was almost ten o'clock in the morning. He thought he heard footsteps. Still, the closeness calmed everything down. But he realized that he did not want to hear anyone. After work, Christian went home. While he was at home, his girlfriend was cooking dinner. She thought of her aunt, Titiana who talked to Christian yesterday. Christian was still interested in the suggestion that Yolanda's aunt hinted at. But he did not indicate that he wanted Yolanda to tell him about it. He remains silent. In the meantime, Siegfried smoked a cigar at home. He was alone. He lay on the armchair. Siegfried felt a little exhausted. He had a long day at the laboratory where he was overseeing the work of Christian. He nevertheless had high hopes for Christian.

It was almost half past eight at night. Sabina watches the television. Since the last production was made, a large audience was enthusiastic about the seductive theme. She received an email from Tatiana. She was a little worried because Christian was considering the new proposal. As long as the preconditions were reasonable, Tatiana was sure that Christian would take up the role again. Nevertheless, there were still some more vacancies that Christian could fill. Sabina closed the remote. Then, she went into a different room. She wrote an email back to Tatiana. After a while, she drank a cup of milk and went to bed.

Chapter 3

Christian was at the doctor's. It was nine o'clock in the morning. He was in pain and had a high temperature. His girlfriend was also ill, but she was at home. He waited for the secretary in reception. A mother with two children walked into the room. The younger child looked at Christian and became tearful. The mother was glancing at him and frowning. The older child was elbowed. Her young brother started to cry again. "Good morning," said Penelope, the receptionist.

"I have an appointment that I made yesterday," said Christian.

"Please come in," said Penelope. She showed Christian into the doctor's room. Christian saw Dr Ned, an elderly man of about seventy years old. ·

"Good morning, Christian," greeted Dr Ned.

"Good morning, Doctor Ned," said Christian.

"Please sit down on the chair," said Dr Ned. He took his Christian's temperature and examined his throat. He looked at Christian and said, "You have flu. Because you have the flu, you should have stayed in bed and drink more water. I would give you a doctor's note and some Panadol. At least you should not have to work for two days. Take two Panadol every six hours."

Christian said, "Thank you, Doctor Ned."

Christian strolled to the building's exit. He flagged down a cab on the street. Still, there was a traffic jam. It was almost half past ten in the morning. Christian reached home after his appointment. He staggered into bed and lay there. After sleeping for an hour or so, Christian got up and went to the fridge where he opened it and took out some orange juice. He poured himself a cup of orange juice and drank it. He took the Panadol that he got from Dr Ned's office. He sat down on the couch in the living room and turned on the television. He watched the news and a cooking show. He looked at his phone but he received no texts from Yolanda. He walked slowly back to his bed and lay there until the afternoon. He then made himself some sandwiches and ate them. In the evening, Yolanda came to visit him. She was feeling much better. She told him of her Aunt Tatiana's impending film where there would be some vacancies that may suit Christian. Christian said that he was feeling a little bit better now. He said that he would visit her Aunt Tatiana soon at the studio. Although he was still feeling a little weak, he was not looking forward to his meeting with Tatiana whom he did not really like. But he tried not to show it as he did not want to offend Yolanda. Although he did not have anything against Tatiana, he was somewhat a little jealous that Yolanda was spending so much time with Tatiana.

Meanwhile, at the studio, Manfred with a bag enters the office. Sabina glanced at him and was speechless. It is midday. "When are you interviewing the candidates?" he asked her.

"I don't know because I need to talk to Tatiana about the roles again," said Sabina.

"That suits me because I could revisit the construction site this week. I'll wait for the result," said Manfred. Manfred was constructing the stage. He had acquired a job to help out in the construction of the stage from the company that owned the studio. He was now a workman with a salary.

"That's no problem. Maybe you can check with me again the next day," said Sabina.

"Thank you very much," said Manfred.

"See you later!" said Sabina.

Manfred walked out of the office to the elevator. The surprising thing between Sabina and Manfred was that they briefly dated each other when Sabina was twenty-two years old. Manfred had always liked Sabina and he tried to tempt her to take the blue ring which he had put on the stone in her pathway. Sabina had then broken off the relationship with Manfred which left him rather sad. Sabina knew that she had to perform well in her job as her boss Tatiana looked upon her very highly. She did not want to disappoint Tatiana. But she also knew that she had a soft spot for Christian whom she wanted to introduce more roles for him. Meanwhile, Christian is back in the old building where there is a laboratory where he worked. He is interested in the geological description of 'The Wonderful World', a book which he had been reading. However, he did not have time to continue reading the entire book. It is almost noon. An hour later, he finished his work and went outside the room. Suddenly, he saw his boss, Siegfried, standing opposite him. Surprisingly, they were now sitting opposite each other. "How do you do?" said Christian politely.

"Please read the instructions I received this parcel today. Please plant the vegetables and get started right away," said

Siegfried handing him over a parcel. Before that, Siegfried read the instructions and looked attentively at the parcel for a while. Christian went into the laboratory with the parcel. He opened the parcel carefully and saw some seeds. He planted the seeds in a test tube and left it there in the laboratory. The seeds would germinate into plants that were needed for an experiment. Siegfried, like Christian, was interested in the sciences and acting. Sometimes, Siegfried would watch a play or two. He had watched the first play in which Christian was asked to dance on the stage. He and Tatiana used to go out for a while. That was also why Siegfried often went to plays as Tatiana kept him abreast of the latest show production that the studio was in charge of. Siegfried was a very serious man who did not talk very much. He lived alone in a house on the periphery of the city centre. In the evening, he would smoke a cigar. He knew that Manfred had been hired by Tatiana to build the construction of the stage. He hoped that Manfred would be able to do a good job in building the construction.

Manfred wrote a novel earlier. Two years earlier, he wished he could have met Sabina again. While he was unemployed, he would meet Sabina in a class at the museum. Manfred owned the blue ring for a long time. He was curious as to its origin and often went to the museum to ask the janitor there. The janitor there got so frustrated with Manfred that he referred him to the museum official who did not have any idea where the ring came from either. To Manfred, it was an ancient ring and had some significance. Although he read the newspapers, he often attended premieres. Nevertheless, he was not at all interested in the current events of the news, but he always thought about them. He had too much to do. He sat down on the armchair. It was ten o'clock in the evening.

Because he was tired, he didn't see anyone on the street. He now lived on the second floor, in the same building as Christian. He did not like his girlfriend, Yolanda who visited Christian. But he did not know that Tatiana knew that he did not like Yolanda as Yolanda had complained to her aunt that she met a rude man, Manfred. It was hushed in the whole building. Christian was not home yet. He was writing a letter to Sabina in his office. Sabina had already drunk a cup of tea that was on her bedside table. Sabina wanted to talk to Tatiana earlier in the day, but she had no results in the role plays. Still, Sabina was disappointed that she was not successful in enlisting Christian for a role play.

Manfred stopped his letter to Sabina. He was determined to pursue her again. He still had the blue ring that Sabina had given Christian. The museum did not answer him. He was frustrated at the same time. He was still annoyed that Sabina had given Christian the ring earlier on. Manfred wanted to ask the museum about the blue ring and to see if they knew where it came from. Manfred was doubtful that the museum knew for he had acquired it in a second-hand shop. Meanwhile, Sabina looked at her wristwatch. It was half past ten in the evening. Manfred went to the cows next to the apartments. He stood by his cowshed and drank a beer. He heard a car driving along the road. He looked out the window. He saw Christian going into the building, which had no garden. He was alone. His girlfriend visited Tatiana today. But Yolanda's cell phone was broken. She was supposed to meet Christian today but because her phone was kaputt, she did not meet Chrisitan as she was uncontactable. Christian looked angry. Manfred stepped away from the window and sat at the table. He turned on his computer. But he had not received any email. Although he had an appointment in the morning with Sabina, she was forgetful and did not attend the meeting with him. It was eleven o'clock in the evening.

Sabina woke up at half past seven in the morning. Meanwhile, Manfred was sleepless all night. He drank beer from morning till night. He gained ten kilos in a year. He straightened his shirt. He went to the office by car. Sabina worked at her computer. Tatiana sat down on the chair in the other room. She picked up her handbag. Her niece, Yolanda spent the night at Tatiana's apartment and did not visit Christian. Christian was still angry. He did not answer his phone. Yolanda had gone to the studio. It was her first day as a scriptwriter. She arrived late. Tatiana smiled at her and continued with her work. Tatiana was eating a piece of carrot. Yolanda used to look after the children. She applied for another job six months later because she was tired of being a nanny as the children made a lot of noise. She had a cup of tea. Meanwhile, Tatiana had outsourced a piece of work to Ulrich who lived in another city. She spoke to Ulrich on the phone. Ulrich informed her that Manfred did not come to work. "What time was he supposed to be there?" she asked.

"I don't know. Maybe Manfred will come the next day because he may not be feeling well," said Ulrich.

"That's a pity. Although we have a special theatrical role, Christian isn't sure yet either," said Tatiana.

"I could do a thorough investigation first-hand because I'm looking forward to the improvements you'll get after lunch," said Ulrich.

"Thank you, that suits me fine," said Tatiana. Ulrich put down the phone. Yolanda was touchy and was working alone. She was lost in thought. Tatiana looked out of the window.

The niece stopped her work and looked around. It was still raining. It was half past ten in the morning. Tatiana went into the kitchen. Yolanda continued to work in the office. Yolanda was very protective of Christian and she knew that despite her working so late in the office every night, she would not cheat on him for she loved him. Christian, on the other hand, was very fond of Yolanda who had a fresh and youthful face.

Yolanda, her niece, is about twenty-eight years old. She had green eyes and long hair. She had known Christian for almost two years. During their friendship, she also danced. Although he would succeed, he learned the foxtrot before the performance, which he practised with Yolanda every day for two months in an artist's studio. Two weeks earlier, they had gone on an outing, but Yolanda was not at all interested in modern art. Christian was a bit disappointed. But Yolanda always talked about her aunt, which he did not really like. He still felt bored in the museum. Christian was at the city centre with Yolanda in a museum. He saw Manfred in another nearby cafe, but he did not look at Christian. A moment later, Manfred had gone outside. Manfred was standing near the bus stop smoking a cigarette. From his left, he could see a dainty ornamental garden; there stood Sabina, who was waiting. Christian followed Manfred. Yolanda looked around the room and noticed that Christian was going out. She was standing alone. Yolanda looked at the painting hanging on the wall. Shortly after, she read the panel describing the picture. She hesitated to follow after Christian. Christian got angry when he saw Manfred and Sabina talking in the park. Manfred looked amused. Sabina was annoyed about the ring. Manfred looked at her. He gave her the ring. Suddenly, she was motionless. Manfred ran away again. Before he left, he said, "If you want, write to me."

Sabina looks unquestioningly at him. She strolled to the bus stop. It was six o'clock in the evening. Yolanda was standing outside the café. She saw the branch office she had been looking for, for a long time standing in the corner. *A white second-story building with lots of windows*, she thought. She saw no one in the park. Christian was calm again. He paid attention to her surprised expression. Earlier, he saw Manfred giving a lecture to Sabina, but at the same time, he looked powerless. He thought about his conversation with Tatiana when she talked about Sabina last week. He was not surprised by what he saw. Then he saw Yolanda. He was walking to the cafe. Christian and Yolanda both ordered their dinner. Sabina got on the bus. She walked home from the bus stop near her apartment. Christian on the other hand took the train home. He was tired and exhausted. It was almost seven o'clock in the evening.

The next day, Yolanda worked in the room. It was half past nine in the morning. Tatiana arrived late. She sees a paper on her table. She was looking for her glasses in her handbag. Yolanda was restless. She was writing. Tatiana read the paper. She put the papers on her table. She wrote her name on the paper and went to another room where Sabina was working. The paper contained the names of the people who would be attending a special play on Sunday. Sabina looked very tired.

"There is nothing new in this publication that I find interesting. The topic is too old-fashioned. Are you getting this from Ulrich at the latest?" Tatiana asked Sabina.

"I have one, but I would have to read the other one first. Christian is coming at noon," replied Sabina.

"That works. Here's the paper; we could do it all on Sunday," said Tatiana.

"Thank you," says Sabina. Tatiana walked out of the room. Sabina felt bad and continued to work. There would be another play on Sunday which Siegfried would be attending. Sabina felt bad because Tatiana had to outsource the work to Ulrich. Nevertheless, she felt compelled to finish the old work which she had left untouched for a week.

It was two o'clock in the afternoon. Sabina looked up and saw Christian standing by the door. "Please wait," Sabina said and walked out of the reception. Christian sat down on the armchair. He looked tired and made himself a cup of coffee from the coffee machine. Tatiana was carrying a lot of paper and a dark book. Nevertheless, she entered the room. Both Tatiana and Christian were sitting at the table. "We have a role you're interested in," said Tatiana.

"I'm looking forward to it," said Christian. C read the book which contained the script.

"Do you have any questions?" asked Tatiana.

"Not really. I'm also coming on Sunday," said Christian. "That's fine. In the same square, by the white building, nine o'clock in the morning," said Tatiana.

"See you later," said Christian and he left the room.

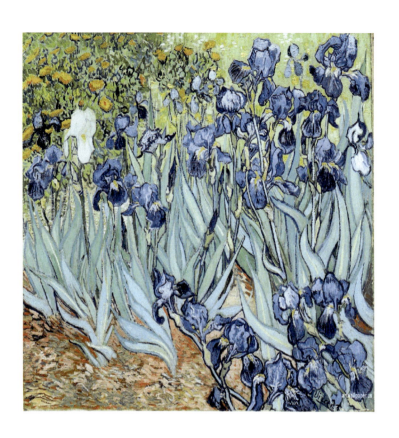

Chapter 4

Christian woke up at eight o'clock. He went to the bathroom. After breakfast, he went to the bus stop. Then he got on the bus. He waited for Yolanda, who had not yet arrived. He saw no one except the white building. He must have had a dreamy night. Still, he was pretty tired. Yolanda drank a cup of tea in the nearby cafe. She saw Christian waiting. Sabina and Tatiana arrived in the vicinity. Both women were cheerful. Christian felt a bit embarrassed because he also saw Yolanda. Siegfried was not annoyed about his work yesterday, he talked to him about it. "You've got a good chance," he said. Because he remembered the result that Christian got after the whole day. He was also in a good mood. Siegfried wanted Christian to put in another scientific article in the magazine. He wanted Christian to get the prize for being the best article writer.

"Good morning," said Siegfried.

"Good morning," said Sabina.

"Hello," said Tatiana. Christian was speechless. Yolanda was touched. She stood opposite him and looked at her wristwatch.

"Here they come," said Sabina.

Many older men and women walk to the white building. Then, the theatrical rehearsal began. Siegfried was interested in the art, but he was not happy with Christian. Sabina felt a bit offended. The weather was nice. It was half past nine in the morning. Christian was also tired. There was no one on the street. All the people were sitting in armchairs in the café. They were drinking and looked happy. Manfred was standing by the chair in the park. He was smoking. He was also touchy. In the meantime, he read the newspapers.

Sabina read the script and stood near the stage. Christian sat down on the chair. He is expressionless. Then he spoke his lines. The movie director looked impressed. Siegfried talked to Sabina for a moment and then went home. Tatiana looked excited. Manfred felt briskly alone. Sabina was not surprised because she knew he was just doing a bit of work. But the building site suited Tatiana fine. Manfred continued to read the newspapers. He appeared to be not working for some time, and Manfred got a little bit lazy. The movie director was unimpressed with Manfred and wanted something to be done to the stage. Suddenly, it was raining. All the people stopped and went to their houses. It was already past midday. Christian went home, too. Yolanda arrived at her house. She cooked. Then she worked. Tatiana and Sabina got on the bus. They were both going to the office. Yolanda was working at home. Christian had arrived. But he went into the room. He felt very uncomfortable. He read the script that Yolanda wrote. He did not like Tatiana's script because Tatiana did not get a copy from Ulrich, who lived in the other city, as Ulrich was known to be a very good scriptwriter.

Christian was working in his room. It was early in the morning. The weather was quite cold. He saw a plant that he cleaned. He was very curious. He did more work, but he got no results. There was a problem with its colour; it did not suit him because he would not have any suitable solutions. "It was pretty much the same," said Siegfried.

"But I'm done," said Christian.

"You would have to do more work," replied Siegfried. His expectations annoyed Christian that he wanted to work him into the whole day. Yet he wanted to leave in the digits, which Christian still did not get. An hour later, Christian went to the street. He bought the newspapers. Then he went for a walk to the old building. He continued to work. It was eleven in the morning. He felt quite cold. He closed the window. There was no noise. He also felt untouched. He read the newspapers for half an hour, but he was not interested in what was in the papers. Because he was trying to find the magazine that Heinrique was selling in the bookshop, he continued to work. He stopped work after midday. Then he had a cup of tea. It was a complicated relationship between Siegfried and Christian who seemed to be working for longer and more hours at the laboratory. On one hand, Siegfried wanted Christian to succeed in his career but on the other hand, he seemed to keep him for so many hours in the laboratory at the expense of his relationship with Yolanda.

It was evening. Christian paid for the ticket at his own expense. But Yolanda had already taken the bus to the theatre. She waited outside the theatre. She strolled to the entrance. Christian had arrived. It was late. They sat on the seats. Christian was not at all interested in the artist because the dancing was too slow. Although she could dance, her dance partner missed a step. Still, he strolled. *It's boring*, thought Christian. Half an hour later, they both went home. Christian felt tired. Yolanda drank a cup of tea and read the newspapers that Christian bought today. She went into another room and continued working on a piece of work which Tatiana had been expecting for a long time. Both were very tired. Christian did not speak. An hour later, she went home. He looked out the window. It was late in the evening. Yolanda did not want to disappoint her Aunt Tatiana and she hoped that she would be able to come up with a script as good as Ulrich.

Early in the morning, Christian went to the old building. There was a bag in his room that belonged to Yolanda. Yolanda was already in the office, but she was not carrying it. Outside the door was a strange woman whom he did not know. He looked at her, then continued working. He felt very restless. He felt a bit untouched. "Excuse me, do you know where Mr Siegfried is?" asked Katharina.

"He's not here yet. It would be best if you waited on the second floor. There's the restaurant," replied Christian.

"Thank you very much," said Katharina.

Christian continued to work. Then he stopped doing his work. Katharina went from his room to the kitchen.

Katharina drank a cup of tea. It was her first day; she sat down on an armchair and read the magazine. After a while, Sabina went into the kitchen. She looked at her for a short moment. Katharina looked very surprised. It was already half past nine in the morning. It was raining outside the window. "Can I help you?" asked Sabina.

"I'm the new assistant," said Katharina.

"Please wait. Mr Siegfried will be late," said Sabina.

"That's fine, thank you," said Katharina. Katharina continued reading the magazine. Sabina left the kitchen. Katharina was not used to people staring at her which she considered rude. She just simply did as she pleased. She was also an only child and had a lot to look forward to in life. She had come to Munich as an intern and had to put up with Yolanda who, on the other hand, was not very fond of her.

It is a nice day. Two weeks later, Tatiana got her revised script which Ulrich gave her. Yolanda and Katharina were working in the same room. Christian had already left. He worked in the office at least two days a week because Sabina preferred to stay at home. "I'd rather you didn't talk too much," said Yolanda to Katharina. Katharina held her cell phone and walked out of the room. She looked bratty. It was in the evening. Katharina met up with Christian in the city centre because she is also the new resident who lives in the same apartment as Yolanda.

"Where is Yolanda?" asked Christian.

"I don't know," replied Katharina.

"Maybe she'll be late," said Christian.

"We should wait here. The train is always late," said Katharina.

Christian went to the bookshop, searching for Heinrique. He finally found the man reading. He looked at Christian, and then Christian entered the shop. Meanwhile, Katharina was waiting alone in the cafe. She looked at her watch and looked very impatient. Then she drank a cup of tea.

Yolanda carried her bag and then sat by the window. The train had gone fast, but she saw Tatiana talking to Siegfried, who was sitting at the front. It was almost half past six in the evening. Although she was curious, she stayed quiet because it was evening. Strangely enough, she found them both cute. Because she had been looking after his children all day, they made a lot of noise in the office. Nevertheless, the passenger train was smokeless. Yolanda arrived. Then she looked for the cafe where Katharina was waiting. It was almost half past seven in the evening. The weather was quite chilly. Yolanda felt a bit cold. She saw Christian coming across the street. In the bookstore, next door is an older man, Heinrique, carrying a bag. He went to the old building where a moving car was already waiting. Siegfried and Tatiana got out of the car. It was almost eight o'clock in the evening. Christian looked a little surprised. "Hello," said Christian.

"Good evening," said Yolanda.

"We're already waiting in the café," said Christian.

"Did you buy the latest magazines?" asked Yolanda.

"No, I only have the newspapers," replied Christian.

"That's a shame," said Yolanda.

"We'll get it in at least two weeks," said Christian.

"That's fine because he's already waiting for the results," said Yolanda.

"Here, this is your ticket. The movie starts in ten minutes," said Christian.

"Let's hurry up," said Yolanda. The two of them walked to the movie theatre. Christian stayed in the cafe. Although Yolanda was not interested in the scientific movie, he sometimes got annoyed by her nonchalance. Yet he paid attention to her expression. Then he saw Katharina, who was waiting. Christian would not have the faintest idea about it. Somewhere, he would have a certainty that she resembled Katharina. Although he was always polite, he did not know her because she remained professional. After an hour, Siegfried was already at home, but Yolanda still wanted to visit her aunt, Tatiana. It was almost ten in the evening. Yolanda had already taken the train to the other town where Tatiana lived. Yolanda was very close to her Aunt Tatiana who looked after her when she was a child. She treated her

Aunt Tatiana with respect for she was her mother's older sister. Aunt Tatiana used to live in another city in the North of Germany but she moved to the South as the weather there was warmer. Yolanda was not the only child in the family. She had two older brothers who were working in the United Kingdom as engineers. However, Yolanda was the youngest in the family and she had always been headstrong. She wanted to excel as a scriptwriter and when she got the job from her Aunt Tatiana, she was overjoyed. She used to look after children as a nanny and she had a lot of experience working with children. Ever since she met Christian, she was very busy with her personal commitments and she gave up her job as a nanny for one of the families. Yolanda's aunt had now moved to the other side of the town and was no longer living in the ground-floor apartment. She sometimes liked to travel to visit her aunt and to see her little cousins for she was a kind person.

Chapter 5

Yolanda arrived at half past nine in the night. Her aunt was waiting in the station room for the whole evening. Yolanda carried a heavy suitcase and walked slower than yesterday. Her aunt was standing opposite.

"Hello," said Tatiana.

"Good evening," said Yolanda.

"I've bought a new car," said Tatiana.

"Where are the children?" asked Yolanda.

"They're at home," said Tatiana.

"We'll drive straight away," said Yolanda.

"That's a good idea," said Tatiana Both women get into the red car. Yolanda looked very happy. It was almost ten o'clock in the evening. There was no one around. It was still raining.

Meanwhile, Christian was reading the newspapers. He thought of his mother, who had not written for a week. It was almost twelve midnight. He went into the bedroom and then looked for a letter he got from his mother. He should also visit her, although he had to buy a ticket. Last week, she moved to another city where she now lives. He went to the kitchen and drank water. Then he slept. Even in his dreams, he thought about his mother a lot.

He went to the station the following day. His train left in ten minutes. He bought the newspapers, then got on the carriage. When he started his journey, it was a sunny day. Yet he was looking forward to the journey, with his mother awaiting his arrival tonight. He drank a cup of tea and looked out the window. There was a forest nearby. Then he wore his glasses and read the newspapers. This express train was the fastest because there was no break. The journey took at least six hours. A man, Lorenzo, the train conductor, was standing opposite. Lorenzo caught his attention. Christian laid the newspapers on the seat. "Ticket, please," said the train conductor. Lorenzo looked at him.

"I only have the monthly ticket," said Christian.

"Are you a student?" asked Lorenzo.

"Yes," said Christian. He nodded and spoke quietly. Lorenzo looked out the window and then looked at his passport for a while.

"Thank you," he said. Christian continued to read the newspapers. The train was moving fast. He could hear the wind blowing against the window. It was still raining. The weather was getting quite cold. It was almost midday. Christian ate an apple and remained indifferent.

It was a quarter past seven in the evening. Christian was standing on the railroad tracks and saw an older man wearing sunglasses. He helped him with his luggage but then did not say a word to him. Christian followed him to his car. "Your mother is already waiting at home," said Babak.

"The weather is cold. The train arrived on time at seven in the evening," said Christian.

"Your favourite car is parked in front," said Babak.

"I'm looking forward to the weekend," said Christian.

"We'll reach the new house. Your father arrives on Saturday. He's in a foreign country at the moment," said Babak.

"Yesterday I wrote him a short letter. This morning, he answered me," said Christian.

"That fits him well," said Babak.

The car drove quickly around a bend. In ten minutes, they reached the widest road. At the end of the road was a massive mansion with a beautifully trimmed garden. He saw his sister, Amelia, standing in front. Amelia, however, was not really his mother. His mother had passed away when Christian was an infant. Amelia happened to be his older half-sister whose mother was Christian's father's first wife. However, Amelia used to take care of Christian when he was a child. That was partly the reason why he had known her to be his mother. Christian knew that Amelia was not his real mother. But there was nothing he could do about calling Amelia his mother. Despite having the irony of calling Amelia his mother, Christian often went to the church where his real mother had been buried. He often thought about his real mother, how kind she was, and how compassionate she was. He was sure that she took care of him from above. He knew that she always stayed close to him. It seemed that it was a very long time since he went to the church again. The worst thing in Christian's life was that he had not seen his real father at all. He was not sure that the father whom he had been corresponding to was his real father. But it seemed real enough for him. He would travel to see his father, he hoped. "Hello," said Amelia. She was carrying a cat.

"Hello, who is this?" asked Christian.

"Emily. She's a Siamese cat I bought today," said Amelia. "She's beautiful," said Christian. He stroke the cat's back.

"Come in. Your room is on the second floor. Thank you, Babak," said Amelia. Babak carried his suitcases into the house.

Christian was alone in his new room. Then he saw his cell phone, which received a text from Yolanda. *Everything is fine. The new script is being printed at the moment. The new, unique role is being approved by Tatiana. Congratulations!* Christian went into the bathroom and drank a glass of water. He sat on a chair and started thinking about the new house. His sister looked delighted, and he was definitely pleased that she looked so good. She used to live in a vast Bavarian house by the river with lots of fish in the south. His sister was a writer and had written many novels. All of her novels were published except for her autobiography, which she left unpublished. His father had worked in the Netherlands since his childhood as an art dealer, collector, and patron of the Van Gogh Foundation. Like his mother, he loved art. On the other hand, Christian had a scientific mind but enjoyed art and drama. His sister was proud of his success as an actor, and he occasionally accepted occasional roles from Sabina's office. His latest script met with the approval of Tatiana and Sabina, which Yolanda had previously passed on to him.

Christian was sitting at the table waiting for his dinner. It was half past six in the evening. His sister, Amelia, walked into the room. She was wearing an expensive dress and a sapphire necklace.

"Good evening, Mother," said Christian.

"Good evening, Christian," said Amelia.

"Where has father been all week?" asked Christian.

"He's attending a conference in Stockholm," said Amelia. "I didn't know he was in Sweden the whole time," said Christian.

"He was forced to be at the conference because he was running it. There was to be an art exhibition in Stockholm at the end of this year that will highlight Van Gogh's collections as well as Impressionist paintings," said Amelia.

"That's exciting! Were you going to be at the exhibition then?" asked Christian.

"Maybe. But if I could go to the city, I would be happy for you to join me at the exhibition," said Amelia.

"That's certainly a great idea. I'll come with you," said Christian. They ate their dinner. Then Christian told his sister a joke about a colleague at his workplace. Amelia laughed at the incident. It was almost eight in the evening. They left the dinner table and went to their respective rooms. Christian was very happy to see his sister looking so radiant. He was to join his sister to go to Stockholm to see the exhibition where he hoped to see his father. He knew that it would be a big moment for him.

Chapter 6

Six months later, Christian was back in the old metropolis with many old buildings where he was working on another project for Siegfried. He ran a role-playing game in the new production in his spare time, which Yolanda had promoted. Meanwhile, Yolanda was pleased with the good reviews that Sabina's and Tatiana's company had received over the months. Christian was looking forward to his trip to Stockholm, where he was going to meet his sister. The relationship that Christian and his sister, Amelia, shared was unique. It allowed Christian to pursue his passion for acting, and this made his sister his closest confidant. However, the two were looking forward to the summer exhibition in Stockholm, where they agreed to go on an adventurous trip over the Christmas period. There, his father could work with the local art museums to open an art exhibition of Van Gogh's most valuable paintings to the public. Christian felt very energized as he worked with the scientific standards that Siegfried had set as rules. Because he had set rigorous standards, Christian worked for long hours every day. Of course, Siegfried remained very pedantic because he carefully reviewed the works of Christian and his other colleagues. Christian displayed an introverted persona but continued to see Yolanda weekly. Meanwhile, the relationship between Christian and Yolanda was growing from strength to strength. The two were planning to get married in a few years' time when they both saved enough. By now, Yolanda had known Christian for almost four years and they were a good couple together. Yolanda wanted to have a lot of children with Christian who was a little apprehensive because he did not really like children. However, with her experience as a nanny looking after children, Christian was confident that she would be able to look after them with him together to the best of their ability.

Sabina met Christian in a café and talked to him about the possibility of shooting a movie in the south of France. "It would be a highlight of your career! We've secured our rights under the script, which would allow us to change it. Her part would be exactly what you've always wanted as a participant in a cycling marathon on the outskirts of town," said Sabina. It took some time to convince Christian. Despite Sabina's enthusiasm, he had already made his trip his priority. Sabina gave him a reassuring smile, then said, "Don't worry, it won't start until the end of next year. We would still be managing the logistics as it would take some time for the sites to be ready."

"That suits me," Christian replied rather quietly.

Sabina, being Christian's acting agent had put him forward as an actor in a real movie to be shot at the South of France. Christian, by now, also had a lot of personal commitments to fulfil. For once, he had to go to Stockholm where he had hoped to see his father and to meet up with Amelia, his sister again. Amelia had meanwhile taken a flight to Stockholm and is touring on her own. Christian was to meet

Amelia in a hotel there and to visit the museum where it was rumoured that his father was working. Amelia arrived in Stockholm and went to the hotel. She had lunch in a cafe of fish and potatoes. She sat in the cafe and had a cup of coffee. She felt a little tired and jet-lagged but she waited for Christian to arrive. In the evening, Christian had taken a flight from Munich to Stockholm. It was a journey lasting for about six and a half hours. Christian was exhausted when he finally reached Stockholm. He was excited as it would be the first time he wanted to see his father. Christian had not seen his real father and did not know what he looked like. But he knew that his real father was a scientist, just like him. He took a taxi to the hotel where Amelia was waiting for him. When he saw his sister, they hugged and went for dinner. They had beef with potatoes and some red wine. After dinner, they were feeling exhausted and they went back to the hotel. In the morning, Christian had a quick shower and changed into his shirt and slacks. He had breakfast with Amelia at the hotel in Stockholm. After that, they took a short tour of the city.

Shortly after lunch, Amelia and Christian took the train to the Sven Harry's Konstmuseum where it was said by Amelia to Christian that his father was working. True enough, Christian saw an elderly man at the museum and thought that it was his father. Amelia said that it was not his father. Christian was very disappointed and felt like crying. Amelia comforted him.

Amelia and Christian, were standing on the second floor of Sven Harry's Konstmuseum and took a look at the painting 'The Starry Night'. When Christian saw the painting, he thought of the suffering and turmoil Van Gogh experienced in his life. He looked calmly at his sister for a moment, then back at the painting. Ten minutes later, the two of them walked to the exit door. As they walked to the exit to get their coats, he told himself to be strong. They left the museum and walked towards a café. The weather was cool but sunny. They sat on an armchair in the café, and then Amelia talked about the extent of the exhibition. Christian still hadn't seen his father. He was expected to be in town in the evening. A moment later, Christian looked at his cell phone. There were still no messages. It was now three in the afternoon in Stockholm. His father had not turned up. Christian was feeling upset as he had been waiting for his father to show up at the museum. He knew that his father was a busy man and perhaps had prior engagements. Amelia put a hand on his shoulder and said to him, "Christian, there is something I wanted to let you know. Our father is no longer alive. We have been trying to cover that fact as we did not want you to be upset. He died almost twenty-five years ago."

"That can't be true," said Christian, feeling very upset.

"What about all the texts and letters he has written to me?" said Christian.

"I am really sorry," said his sister, Amelia.

"I know that I am not your real mother either. Just your sister," said Amelia.

"I did not want to hurt you. But I know that you deserved the truth," said Amelia.

"What about all the people that I worked with? Do they deserve the truth too?" said Christian.

"I am really sorry, Christian. Siegfried is your uncle. He is the only man in the world closest in blood to our father," said Amelia.

"Oh dear!" exclaimed Christian.

"I must talk to him again for he is our uncle," said Christian.

With that, both Amelia and Christian decided to leave Stockholm and go to the airport where they both took a flight back to Germany. It seemed that Christian had acquired some truth to his parentage which many had not known about. At least, as an only child, he was free to make decisions that may impact him positively. For he knew that he had to stand firm with his sister in life and that together, they would discover what their real father would be like in real life. It was very important for Christian that he be told the truth, for at least, he knew where he stood in life. His career as a scientist and an actor would blossom. He was to return to the South of France again to film his new movie. He knew that he had a future with Yolanda whom he was very fond of. Christian had to accept the truth that was being told to him and that with the truth, he would then be able to forge his integrity as a man. It was important for Christian to be able to forge his identity as a man for it meant that he would be able to form a realistic relationship with Yolanda. As he was very close to Amelia, Christian no longer called her his mother, in fact, he called her his sister. Amelia did not want to lose Christian which is why she made him call her his mother when in fact she was his sister. Today, he learnt that his real father had died so many years ago, which was a personal shock to him. However, his real father was very rich and he did not die penniless. He had left to Amelia and Christian his large fortune which was being held in trust for the both of them. With some payment from their trustees, Amelia was able to buy a house in the North of Germany and Christian was able to buy an apartment from the city centre in Munich. His real father had a vast collection of paintings too which he had given to Christian. With his love of art and painting, Christian was sure to take good care of the paintings. It would be a testimony to his cultural heritage as well and for the many years to come, he and Yolanda would have a family of their own. Both Yolanda and him would go on to have five children. Christian and his family would move to the Bavarian Alps where they would have a huge mansion. As Christian was a very introverted person, Yolanda would complement him in his personality in that she would be the first to find out what was bothering him in his personal moments. Their three girls and two boys would learn the trade of art and painting now that the trustees had released these paintings to Christian. They would be a very close family and as Christian has always been the only child of his mother, he would always treasure Yolanda and his children.